My Navajo Sister

by Eleanor Schick

Simon & Schuster Books for Young Readers

SIMON & SCHUSTER BOOKS FOR YOUNG READERS
An imprint of Simon & Schuster Children's Publishing Division
1230 Avenue of the Americas
New York, New York 10020
Copyright © 1996 by Eleanor Schick
All rights reserved including the right of reproduction
in whole or in part in any form.
SIMON & SCHUSTER BOOKS FOR YOUNG READERS is a trademark of Simon & Schuster.
Book design by Anahid Hamparian
The text of this book is set in 19-point Caxton
The illustrations are rendered in colored pencil
Manufactured in the United States of America
First Edition
10 9 8 7 6 5 4 3 2 1
Library of Congress Cataloging-in-Publication Data
Schick, Eleanor.
My Navajo sister / by Eleanor Schick.
p.   cm.
Summary: A white girl lives for a short time on an Indian reservation and
forms a close bond with a Navajo girl.
1. Navajo Indians—Juvenile fiction.   [1. Navajo Indians—Fiction. 2. Indians of North America—
Fiction. 3. Friendship—Fiction.] I. Title
PZ7.S3445Myn 1993
[Fic]—dc20   91-39073
ISBN: 0-689-80529-2

For Genni

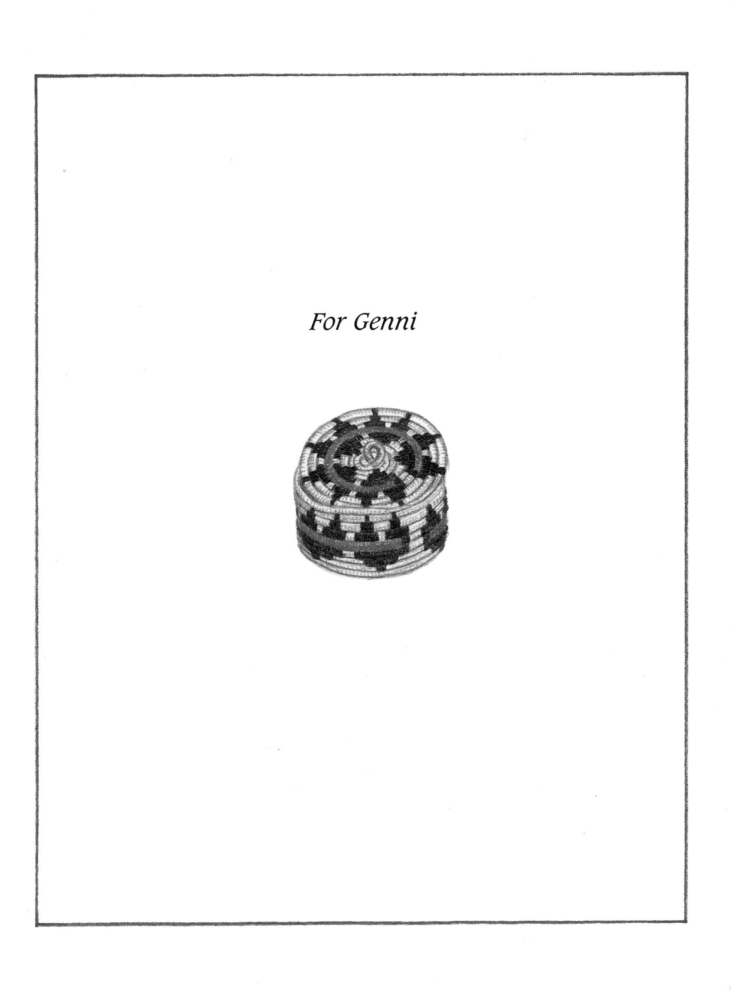

Genni, when I came with my family to live on Navajo land, you made me feel welcome. You invited me to your home and on the very first day I visited, you gave me a basket.

That summer, we walked the back roads, you and I. We pretended we were sisters and it was long ago, before there was a reservation.

We climbed the canyon walls and collected shells left by the sea—maybe thousands or millions of years ago. You told me that the spirits of your people from long ago still live there. You called them the Ancient Ones.

One time we couldn't help falling asleep in one of the caves. When we woke up, we told each other our dreams. Yours was that the Ancient Ones came to visit us. Mine was the same, and they welcomed me to Navajo land. You smiled when I told you that, like you already knew.

We stayed at your grandmother's ranch.
You showed me her horses, running free in
the canyon. We wanted to ride them.

We tried to catch Pepper, the gentle one, but she kept getting away. Yago, the big, strong, stubborn one, nuzzled up close. "We'll ride Yago together!" we decided. Your brother warned us not to. We laughed and told him not to worry. He saddled up Yago, but he warned us again.

We rode to the edge of the pine forest, then we turned back. Going home, Yago galloped so fast and hard, he threw us both. We got hurt, and we were scared to come home, because your brother had warned us. Still, your cousin Eunice cleaned our cuts and scrapes, and no one scolded us.

Only one week later, your brother coaxed us
to ride with him. He rode Yago and we rode
Pepper, all the way up the canyon to the
family picnic. That day, while the mutton
roasted in the ground and the beans
cooked in the campfire pot, you and
I collected leaves from the cottonwoods,
turning golden with winter coming.

You teased me for eating just vegetables
and fruits, and your mother named me
Sparrow, saying, "She eats like a bird!"
All the family said, "That's your Navajo
name, now." And from that day on, it was.

Later that winter, your cousin Tina got married. We sat on the hogan floor while the medicine man chanted blessings. Everyone ate some cornmeal from the wedding basket.

We sisters had spent days helping to prepare the feast. After the ceremony, we served the guests. I remember how you and I spilled the whole bowl of punch, trying to carry it by ourselves. We hoped the wedding guests wouldn't see how we laughed and laughed, because we were so embarrassed.

The next day, Tina's mother gave us each a gift. Mine was a silver bracelet with turquoise, more beautiful than I had ever seen. She said, "It is our custom to give gifts from the wedding dowry to the women of the family who make the wedding feast." That day she said I became one of the women of the family.

Genni, we lived among your people for so
short a time, and then we moved away.
In that time, you and I became sisters. I
hold the basket now, remembering your soft
voice. I spread out my seashells from the
canyon and the dried, golden cottonwood
leaves. I wear the silver bracelet.

One year passed, and I cried. A second year is passing now, and I am growing strong in the knowledge of what we shared.

I am still your sister, Genni.
I always will be.